Mr. Fooster

Traveling on a Whim

To my lovely neighbor Mary — and your eternal sense of wonder —

[signature]

A Visual Novel

Written by

Tom Corwin

Illustrated by

Craig Frazier

DOUBLEDAY

FLYING DOLPHIN PRESS

New York   London   Toronto   Sydney   Auckland

FLYING
DOLPHIN
P R E S S

PUBLISHED BY DOUBLEDAY / FLYING DOLPHIN PRESS

Published in the United States by Doubleday/Flying Dolphin Press, an imprint of The Doubleday Publishing Group, a division of Random House, Inc., New York.

www.flyingdolphinpress.com

FLYING DOLPHIN PRESS & DESIGN is a registered trademark of Random House, Inc.

Book design by Craig Frazier

Library of Congress Cataloging-in-Publication Data
Corwin, Tom.
  Mr. Fooster traveling on a whim / by Tom Corwin ; illustrated by Craig Frazier.—1st ed.
    p. cm.
1. Graphic novels. I. Frazier, Craig, 1955–ill. II. Title. III. Title: Mister Fooster traveling on a whim.
  PN6727.C674M7 2008
  741.5'973—dc22
                        2007050308

ISBN 978-0-385-52340-0

PRINTED IN THE UNITED STATES OF AMERICA

10 9 8 7 6 5 4 3 2 1

First Edition

1

A Puzzling Pause

Mr. Fooster has a long list of things he likes to do. One is dreaming. Another is looking for arrowheads. On this Tuesday morning he did neither. He simply put an old wrinkled letter back into its envelope, placed it into his coat pocket, and headed out the door with no particular place to go.

As he walked, his mind began to wander. How was it that prophets could manifest things and he couldn't? How come mandarin oranges came in perfect little segments without any mechanical engineering? Why was it that bubbles bobbled to and fro, yet always found their way back to a perfect sphere?

Sooner than later he stumbled on a small rock, which jostled him from his odd meanderings. He looked down and saw a katydid. The katydid did something unusual.

She smiled.

In all his days Mr. Fooster had never seen a katydid smile. It took him quite by surprise, but he pulled himself together quickly and ambled onward. As his mind wandered off again, his feet set a rhythm and he began to whistle to himself.

The spontaneous melody was hypnotic, and before he knew it, it was nightfall and he did not recognize his surroundings.

How could he get back home in time for bed? All he had with him were his compass and an old bottle of bubble soap.

He sat on a stump and waited for the answer. As boredom set in, he pulled out that old bottle of bubble soap, unscrewed the top, and poked around for the little red wand.

As he blew the first bubble, he knew something odd was happening. The bubble just kept coming. And it was not shaping into a sphere, but rather an old DeSoto sedan, exactly like the one his grandfather used to drive.

Just as he reached the end of his breath, the bubble became whole and plopped onto the road in front of him.

Baffled by this apparition, he wallowed in a lazy moment of puzzling pause. Then, following his instinct, Mr. Fooster hopped in and drove the DeSoto home, arriving just in time for bed.

2

In an Instant

In the morning Mr. Fooster lay in bed, gazed at the ceiling, and considered yesterday's outing. Rising from his comfortable cotton sheets, he peeked out the window, squinted, stared, rubbed his eyes, and looked again...lo and behold (whatever that means), there stood the DeSoto, green, shiny, and proud.

Before leaving the house he listed the DeSoto on eBay® in hopes of raising funds for his favorite charity, the Pickle Family Circus.

As he headed out, he checked the compass in his pocket. It pointed north. He headed west with thoughts of swimming to Cambodia.

Over hill and dale he walked with a floating feeling in his step. As he progressed toward the ocean his thoughts traveled to faraway places. Why were ducks so fuel-efficient? How come you never see baby pigeons? Who figured out how to eat artichokes?

Suddenly a very large shadow roused him from his train of thought and he found himself facing a bug the size of a bulldozer. He stared in amazement as the grumpy bug munched on the trunk of a linden tree.

With three orange spots on his forehead and crunching munching sounds from his cavernous mouth, the bug addressed Mr. Fooster.

"I, dear sir, am eating a path around the world. Each day I consume everyone and everything that crosses my trail until I am full. Yesterday I ate a freight train, an oak tree, and a bird whistle. It is endless and serious work, but this is how I must make my mark on the world."

Mr. Fooster appeared to be in hot water.

The big bug continued, "Before I sprinkle some salt on your toes and add you to my lunch menu, I have one question...

"I can see from the lightness in your step that you are traveling on a whim. What makes you so content?"

Mr. Fooster considered the question as a flock of ducks passed overhead. He could hear the wind under their wings. Unsure how to address the big bug, he instinctively reached into his pocket and pulled out his bubble soap.

He dipped his fingers into the thick, soupy soap, raised the wand to his lips, and began to blow.

A bubble slowly emerged. It stretched, warped, and swayed this way and that, bobbling and shnobbling, wibbling and wobbling—its enormity became truly baffling.

As it eclipsed the size of the DeSoto and dwarfed the big bug, it struggled to find its final shape.

Alas the bubble broke free of the wand and floated off to the west in the likeness of an immense birdcage filled with vibrant floating tropical fish. As it reached the horizon, the cage door opened and all the beautiful fish swam out and soared into the clouds.

The big bug smiled so wide that his joy lifted him into the air. In an instant he saw the silliness of his seriousness, and in his reverie, he too floated off into the horizon.

As he disappeared into the skyline, the tracings of two jubilant words were heard erupting from his mouth: "Chili mambo!"

Mr. Fooster watched with a curious look on his face and continued on his journey.

3

Belly First

Three days passed as Mr. Fooster walked day and night, each step just as light as the one before. He could imagine the ocean breeze and the blue water that awaited just over the next mountain.

Occasionally he would look up from his rambling thoughts and notice something new—the call of a sea-bird, the smell of a juniper bush, or a poker chip left in the dust.

As he neared the next hilltop he stopped to look in a pothole. An exhausted newt gazed back at him and asked for directions to the nearest swamp. From the look in his eyes, Mr. Fooster could tell that the newt was weak.

Hearing the distant sound of running water through the woods to the north, he decided to help. Picking up the newt and placing him on his shoulder, he headed toward the sound of the creek.

With the newt on his shoulder, conversation came easily and telepathically. Their "talk" was heartfelt, deep, and meaningful. The newt's world, it seemed, existed solely of puddles, potholes, and mud.

He had never heard of the ocean, tasted salt water, or seen a sailboat, but was determined to quest out into the wilds beyond, to prove his strength and importance to the other newts in the marsh.

The cacophony of frogs chattering in the distance gave assurance that Mr. Fooster was closing in on the bog.

Coming upon a mud puddle, he carefully placed the newt in, belly first.

As he turned to head back to the road, he noticed how perfect and stinky the newt's swamp was.

Another day passed before Mr. Fooster's shoes touched the sand. As he stepped to the water's edge, he gazed at his reflection.

His desire to swim had passed, but a rowboat called out to him. He stepped in, took the oars, and headed off for a better look at the horizon.

The water shimmered with the reflection of the sun, as if he were rowing through a big pot of gold.

As he settled into a comfortable pace, he considered why bathtubs were always too short for comfort, how come the letter *p* was included in the word *psychology*, and what a burden gravity was when you had to move an oven.

As he pondered, he noticed his rowing became easier and lighter. The heat of the sun warmed his back. And the day took on a deeper meaning.

Time passed easily as he floated to the beach and returned the rowboat to its mooring. With sea salt on his hat, he faced west one last time.

While he was admiring the orange sunset, some small objects fell from the sky and landed half buried in the sand in front of him. As he looked down he noticed the corner of a tiny wood block. Slowly kneeling, Mr. Fooster pulled a handful of Scrabble® tiles out of the sand and placed them in his pants pocket. Then, reaching out his arms, he gathered up a piece of the ocean to show the newt on his walk home.

4

A Thousand Rotations

Upon his return home, Mr. Fooster went straight to bed. Settling back into his cozy cotton sheets felt so good that he slept for a week.

He dreamed of parsnips, walnuts, feathers, and fruit, dogs that were fish, and a bird that played the ukulele. He rode on a carpet across the sea and collected a bowl full of smiles before awakening the following Wednesday.

As he wandered toward wakefulness he noticed that the crisp, clear air carried a hint of the changing seasons. The morning dew sparkled in the sun and he felt the impulse to rise and shine.

Before heading out, he paused to review the old letter in his pocket, noticing several words had fallen from the page. Though it was postmarked April 7, 1896, it seemed his great uncle Fooster still had more—or less—to say. With glue stick in hand, Mr. Fooster laid the letter flat, arranged his newfound Scrabble® tiles on the kitchen table before him, and fell into a deep spell of concentration.

As the clock reached the hour, Mr. Fooster opened the front door and was welcomed by the sweet smell of spring. It was a clear invitation for a brisk walk. Feeling the call of the North, he closed the door behind him.

As he walked, he considered many things: Why is yawning contagious? How long do frogs' tongues get? Why do grown-ups lose their sense of wonder?

He came to a sign nailed to the fence by the side of the road that read like a secret map. It had many arrows this way and that and symbols he had never seen before. It stood beside a dark and wooded path. Unable to decipher its code, he headed down the mysterious trail.

At first he walked with a sense of caution, but ultimately found his comfortable, swift pace. As the path progressed, the vegetation became more and more dense until he eventually found himself surrounded by green walls of strange thick-leaved bushes. He continued down the path, taking countless lefts and rights, with no end in sight.

As the hours passed his pace held steady; then out of the blue a resounding cry filled his consciousness: "Stop!" He froze in his tracks and looked around for a clue to this intuition. With one foot still floating just above the ground, he noticed a plump yellow-striped caterpillar on the path right where his foot was about to land. Taking a moment to wallow in its bright, spiky hairdo, he was reminded that life could bring an endless series of surprises. Gently stepping to the side, he proceeded down the path.

Days passed and Mr. Fooster walked on. By the fifth day his compass had spun a thousand rotations. He had walked through a myriad of twists, turns, and spirals. There was not only no end in sight, but, by all appearances, no end at all. Mr. Fooster's feet began to feel heavier with each step.

Standing in the sunlight, he considered his predicament. As he bathed in the warmth of the afternoon light, he felt his shoes begin to tenderly vibrate. When he tried to take another step, he found the soles of his feet were growing roots into the ground.

Aching for Life

Unable to move, Mr. Fooster turned his attention inward. How do ladybugs make baby bugs without manbugs? Can lightning really knock your socks off? Is it possible there is really no word that rhymes with orange?

As his thoughts wandered on, he noticed a prickly sensation in his arms and legs. It was an odd feeling, as if all his limbs were going to sleep at one time. A moment later he began to sprout leaves.

As his leaves grew, a lovely smell, not unlike fresh vine-ripened tomatoes, filled the air.

Over the next few days he grew more accustomed to standing in one place. He watched with curiosity as porcupines and woodchucks passed by, occasionally stopping to sniff his legs.

Every now and then he'd feel the tickle of an earthworm loosening the soil as it slithered under his feet. As his roots grew, Mr. Fooster sensed their hungry search for water and it occurred to him that his journey might be over.

Summer came and went. The brisk fall air whispered of a coming frost. Mr. Fooster's nose grew pink as winter approached. One day the sky turned gray and a big snow covered the forest like a heavy down comforter.

The thick white blanket brought even deeper moments of silence. There was a true hush in the air. Mr. Fooster could feel the rhythms of nature quietly aching to come back to life.

6

A Galaxy Away

From high above, the planet Earth looked like a big beach ball floating in the air. Gazing across the universe, the big bug's neck hairs began standing straight up on end. Overtaken by this odd feeling, he searched his recently lightened heart for what it might be: the first signs of a flu, an approaching electrical storm, or had he rested his head on a patch of poison ivy while lying on his back admiring the sunset?

He tried to distract himself with some playful mind games, hoping the feeling would soon subside. Reciting the alphabet backward as fast as he possibly could didn't help. So he began counting the passing dust particles in the air.

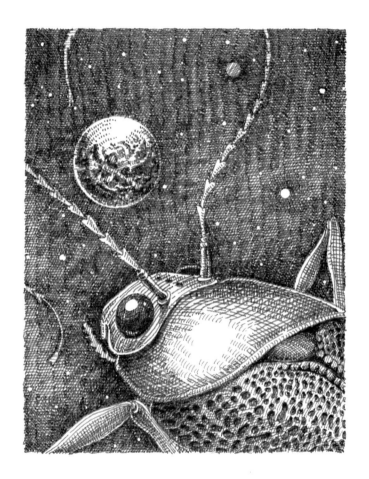

As he reached 97,342 particles, something dawned on him. Actually, it hit him in the head like a well-greased frying pan. It was one of those unexpected moments when you know you know something, but you don't know exactly how you know it…

A *friend was in trouble*. He felt it in his exoskeleton as sure as the moon was blue (which it was).

With this sudden realization came the impulse to help in any way he could. He stopped counting dust particles and headed off toward the feeling.

Speeding through the galaxy, he passed meteors and asteroids, crossed the Milky Way, and continued to follow the scent of his knowing. With Alpha Centauri in his wake, still gaining momentum, he thrust past the crescent moon and onward toward the planet Earth.

The beauty of the approaching orb filled his soul with awe. The bounty of life below infused him with the deepest humility. As his soul expanded, his body began to shrink, assuming a more natural proportion to the wonders of the world.

Entering Earth's atmosphere was a shock to his system. He had forgotten about the burdens of gravity, and for the first few minutes his legs hung like wet laundry from his hips—all six of them.

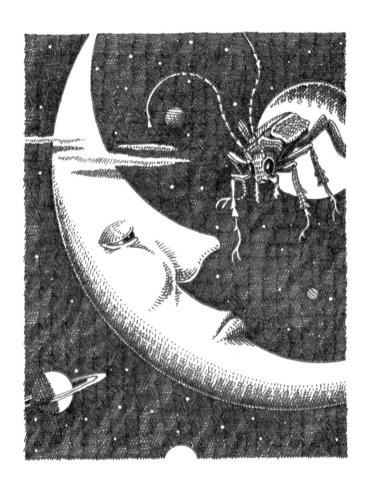

7

Tough to Swallow

As he drew closer to Earth the big bug could feel the pull of a tiny green patch off to the right. Closing his eyes, he saw a blinking bull's-eye clearly calling out to him.

He was falling with the growing speed of a bowling ball, and before you could say "Bob's your uncle," he had landed atop a fine old oak tree and fell to the ground.

After shaking out his confused legs he rolled over and stood up. It took only a minute or two for his sense of pride to return. He was reminded of how foolish he had been before leaving this planet and enjoyed the warm feeling of wisdom now resting in his proverbial bones.

Snow floated in the air like magic fairy dust, but the surrounding area felt as barren as a desert floor. Admiring the still, white tone of the snow-covered garden he stumbled forward, slipping and slopping toward the trusted feeling. There were no footsteps in the whiteness, just soft rounded knobs and hills.

He surveyed the landscape, fully expecting to meet up with a familiar face. Oddly enough, as certain as he was of the sensation, there were no faces to be found, just trees and shrubs as far as the eye could see.

After hours of searching, exhaustion caught up with him.

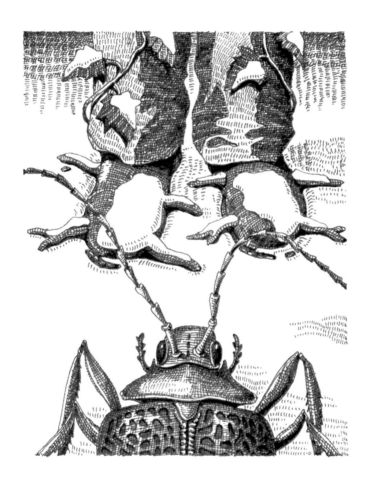

Meanwhile, Mr. Fooster had been watching as the big bug ambled around.

Unable to move, he was resigned to watching life unfold before him. After a few minutes, the gargantuan bug lay down at his feet and took a nap. The company was welcome, but the smell was tough to swallow.

As often happened, Mr. Fooster's mind began to stir. How can you smell a skunk from two miles away, when its spray travels only two yards? If the brain is made of 80 percent water, what might the ocean be thinking? How come it takes more muscles to frown than to smile?

…perhaps we were intended to smile.

Night fell and morning after morning passed. The big bug would occasionally wake up, look around, and go back to sleep. A few times he got up and wandered off in another direction, but, alas, always returned to the same spot before the day was through.

8

A Blissful Blankness

Two more months passed and Mr. Fooster actually began to enjoy the foul smell of the bug. He came to recognize a certain sweetness just beyond the stench.

With the spring thaw, his nose returned to its normal color. And his thoughts stirred with new life. As the sun settled into its midmorning stretch, a butterfly landed on his hat. As it sat there flexing its wings in the sun, Mr. Fooster heard the whisper of the butterfly's voice.

"The ties that bind you are but your own, kind sir. Your imagination has simply forgotten itself. Think yourself free and follow as the wind and my wings lead the way."

At that moment, a soft wind brushed across his face and the butterfly took flight. As the breeze carried the butterfly into the distance, he watched it fly away with the delicacy of a down feather. Mr. Fooster pulled at his feet. His leaves rustled, but he just couldn't lift his soles.

Startled by the movement, the big bug watched in amazement, finally recognizing Mr. Fooster beneath the leaves and branches that surrounded him. Feeling both overjoyed to see him and comforted that his knowing had not led him astray, he smiled so wide he nearly cracked open.

Alarmed by Mr. Fooster's continued stillness, the big bug did the only thing he could think of to communicate with this master of silence.

He reached to the bottom of his big soul and yelled at the top of his lungs. Two small words were set free with the force of a freight train.

"Chili mambo!" The words shook the garden with the resonance of a foghorn.

The force of the big bug's voice shook Mr. Fooster's roots. Recognizing his friend's care and concern, he reconsidered his position. The butterfly was nearly out of sight, but the echoes of its voice filled his head a second time. "Think yourself free…"

Luxuriating in the thought, he took a deep breath. As he exhaled, the butterfly's message rang longer, louder, and true.

As his head filled with a blissful blankness, he was suddenly aware of every molecule of spring. Feeling his connection to all things, he realized he could be happy attached to the ground forever. With this thought the lightness of his soles returned.

With a single step, all his leaves and branches fell to the ground in his own personal change of seasons.

A Great Sense of Pride

The colorful wings of the butterfly were now but a speck in the distant breeze. As he took his first steps Mr. Fooster nodded his head toward the big bug with a sense of gratitude and respect, realizing his company had been a great comfort on the coldest of nights.

The big bug's smile reflected the sun like a solar eclipse, making the fine spring day even brighter. It was not long before Mr. Fooster was following the butterfly's lead.

Although the butterfly flittered and fluttered, Mr. Fooster noticed that it flew with a great sense of pride. When the slightest of breezes blew it off course, it simply steadied itself and followed its path without worry or wart.

In a short time the butterfly led him straight to a huge ivy-covered gate. It was constructed of old withered wood, a crisscrossing of small branches woven together like a tapestry. A large, twisted, lichen-covered branch arched over the gate.

A heavy black iron ring hung where a door handle would be. Mr. Fooster reached through the ivy and turned the large metal ring. As the gate creaked open he stepped through.

10

The Pregnant Pause

Mr. Fooster looked up at a towering stone wall that loomed just beyond the gate. It was made of huge blocks of rough stone and stood twenty feet high. He looked to the right, and the wall appeared to go on forever. Turning to the left, Mr. Fooster decided to follow the wall and see where it led him.

Five, ten, fifteen minutes passed; the wall curved around a few trees and continued. Stepping over an old wheel half stuck in the ground he moved on—forty-five minutes, one hour. As the second hour ticked by, the sound of a hammer began echoing through the trees. As he continued down the path, the sound became louder and louder. He eventually came upon the source.

A small man, no taller than a mulberry bush, was working on the wall. He was so focused on his work, he didn't notice Mr. Fooster approaching. Surrounded by tools, ladders, ropes, and fulcrums to assist in the building of the wall, he was clearly skilled and clever.

His ears must have been numb from the endless crashing of the hammer, for even as Mr. Fooster's foot snapped a stick the small man didn't notice him. When he finally looked up, his face turned from white to a deep red and he simply exploded in anger.

"Who are *you*? How in the world did you manage to pass through *my* labyrinth? I spent seven years designing that to keep everyone out. I have been working for twelve years now to complete this great wall. It will guarantee that *no one* shall ever step into my house again."

"There is nothing worth anything on this earth," he continued. *Grumble, shlumble, trumble.* "I will not be satisfied until the wall is finished and I can close out the world forever." *Grumble, brumble, mumble.* "What excuse do you have for invading my privacy? Tell me before I banish you to the labyrinth forever and lock the gates!"

Mr. Fooster watched with interest as the little man worked himself into a raging tizzy. When he finally stopped grumbling, he punctuated the end of his rant by grandly spitting on the ground in disgust.

A pregnant pause lay between them as the little man watched Mr. Fooster slowly reach into his pocket. The man had expected this tall stranger to run like the others before him, but instead he fished out a harmless little bubble wand from a small bottle and began to blow.

11

A Very Small Miracle

A bubble began to reach out toward the small man. It bobbed and quivered and shmooked and mooked, finding its way into shape. As it completed its form, it snapped off the wand in the likeness of a large magnifying glass.

The bubble floated over to the small man and hovered right in front of his face. As he looked to the right the lens followed in front of him. He stepped backward and forward, left and right—no matter which direction he turned, the magnification brought his attention to his microscopic surroundings.

In a moment his face went blank, then his wrinkled brow relaxed. As he gazed down at his feet he noticed the ground on which he was standing was blanketed with the tiniest purple flowers, each one a small miracle in and of itself.

He gently dropped to his knees, making sure not to harm the flowers, and began to cry. As his tears touched the ground, he watched in wonder as ladybugs gathered to drink this unexpected refreshment.

As Mr. Fooster headed off, he pulled out the old letter in his front pocket. The Scrabble® tiles remained right where he had glued them many months ago.

There are times one must wait for the words to sink in, especially when a few letters are missing. In that moment a certain line fell right into place. "_uestion your assu_ptions and your wor_d too can change."

Looking down, he noticed an old rusted bicycle leaning up against an oak tree.

As he rode off, Mr. Fooster couldn't help but notice the squeaky wheel repeating the butterfly's words: "Think yourself free, think yourself free, think yourself free." Inspired by its rhythm, he began whistling a new melody. As he pondered the next call of his compass, he pedaled straight home.

Also by Tom Corwin
Mostly Bob

Also by Craig Frazier
Trucks Roll!
Stanley Goes Fishing
Stanley Mows the Lawn
Stanley Goes for a Drive
The Illustrated Voice

We would like to express our profound gratitude to Deb Futter, Robert Stricker and Charlotte Sheedy for their infinite faith in Fooster.

This book's text is set in Goudy Oldstyle and produced using Adobe® InDesign® and Photoshop®.

The illustrations were created using a combination of Pigma® Micron® Archival Ink Pens (brown .005 and .01) and Faber-Castell Pitt Artist Brush Nib Pen (sanguine), drawn in Moleskine® Cahier Notebooks. They are printed as duotones using black and PMS 139.